FEAR OF FLYING

Written by Nancy Lambert

Illustrated by Ron Lim and Rachelle Rosenberg

Based on the Marvel comic book series The Avengers

Los Angeles
New York

marvelkids.com

Printed in the United States of America
First Edition, February 2016
1 3 5 7 9 10 8 6 4 2
ISBN 978-1-4847-3200-7
FAC-029261-15352
Library of Congress Control Number: 2015953287

SUSTAINABLE
FORESTRY
INITIATIVE

Certified Sourcing

www.sfiprogram.org
SFI-01415

Falcon is an Avenger.
His partner Redwing is a bird.
Together they fight bad guys.

Falcon and Redwing are flying
over the city on patrol.
A bright red beam cuts through
the clouds.

The beam almost hits Falcon!
Falcon and Redwing look around.
Who shot the beam?

It was Red Skull! He is flying
with a jet pack. He has a powerful
mind-control blaster.

Red Skull fires his new weapon
at Falcon again.

The beam hits Falcon!
Now Falcon is afraid to fly!
Red Skull laughs.

Falcon is falling. He is going to crash. Redwing helps him land.

Falcon and Redwing look out
at the city.

Falcon can see danger in the distance. Red Skull is coming back.

Red Skull sends flying robots
to attack the city.
Falcon wants to stop them,
but he is too afraid to fly.

Falcon tries to fight the robots.
He shoots daggers from his
wings at the robots.

Falcon needs help.
Iron Man joins the fight.

Iron Man blasts the robots apart
with his repulsor beams.

After the fight, Iron Man talks to
Falcon. He tells his friend he can
fly again if he keeps trying.

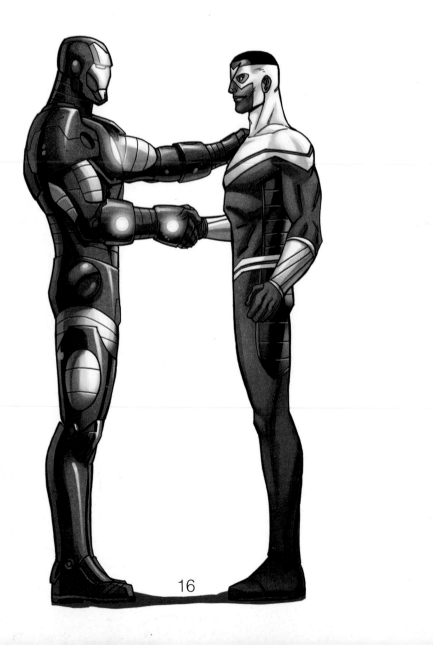

The next day, Red Skull sends
out more flying robots. They
attack the S.H.I.E.L.D. Helicarrier.
Falcon is still afraid to fly.

He uses his falcon talons
to grab the robots.

He can only catch them one at a time. Redwing comes to help.

Captain America joins the battle.
He throws his shield at the robots.

The robots explode in the air.
Captain America and Falcon
stop the robots.

After the battle, Captain America
tells Falcon he will fly again.
Falcon must beat the mind control.

Falcon practices every day.
Redwing helps him. At first,
he cannot fly very high.
He is still too afraid.

The next day, Redwing disappears.
Falcon hears Redwing calling for
help. Red Skull has captured him.
Falcon must fly to save his partner.

Falcon remembers what
Captain America said.
He leaps and flies to Redwing.
He is no longer afraid to fly!

Falcon bursts into Red Skull's hideout. Red Skull is shocked. Falcon defeated Red Skull's mind control.

Falcon goes to Redwing to free him. Red Skull aims the mind-control blaster at Falcon.

The beam hits Falcon. Red Skull's mind control does not work on Falcon anymore!

Falcon fires daggers at Red Skull.
They knock out the villain.
Redwing takes the blaster.

Redwing flies high and drops the blaster. It smashes on the rooftop.

Red Skull's mind-control device
can never be used again.
Falcon takes Red Skull to jail.

Iron Man and Cap are proud of
Falcon. He beat his fear of flying.
Now Falcon and Redwing are
back in the sky, where they belong.